In Singing, He Composed a Song

UNIVERSITY OF CALGARY
Press

In Singing,
He Composed a Song

Jeremy Stewart

Brave & Brilliant Series
ISSN 2371-7238 (Print) ISSN 2371-7246 (Online)

University of Calgary Press
2500 University Drive NW
Calgary, Alberta
Canada T2N 1N4
press.ucalgary.ca

This is a work of fiction. Names, characters, businesses, places, events, and incidents are either the products of the author's imagination or used in a fictitious manner. Any resemblance to actual persons, living or dead, or actual events is purely coincidental.

LIBRARY AND ARCHIVES CANADA CATALOGUING IN PUBLICATION

Title: In singing, he composed a song / Jeremy Stewart.
Names: Stewart, Jeremy, 1982- author.
Series: Brave & brilliant series ; no. 22. 2371-7238
Description: Series statement: Brave & brilliant series, 2371-7238 ; no. 22
Identifiers: Canadiana (print) 20210133244 | Canadiana (ebook) 20210133449 | ISBN
    9781773852201 (softcover) | ISBN 9781773852218 (PDF) | ISBN 9781773852225 (EPUB)
Classification: LCC PS8637.T49455 I5 2021 | DDC C813/.6—dc23

The University of Calgary Press acknowledges the support of the Government of Alberta through the Alberta Media Fund for our publications. We acknowledge the financial support of the Government of Canada. We acknowledge the financial support of the Canada Council for the Arts for our publishing program.

  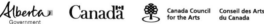

Printed and bound in Canada by Marquis Book Printing
♻ This book is printed on Opaque Smooth Cream paper

Editing by Naomi K. Lewis
Cover image by Erin Arding Stewart
Cover design, page design, and typesetting by Melina Cusano

to my friends

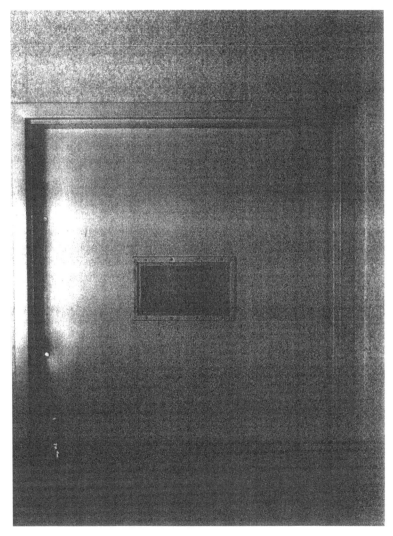

View of the Prince George Regional Hospital
Psychiatric Intensive Care Unit from inside

streets are dry so at last I can
walk anywhere in this town, a full pack of smokes

I find winking moon visions inaccessible by daylight
thinking—zombie power, hands in pockets, mind turning over

some daydream, nothing but this sleepwalking prayer
& the search for friends.

Anguished at the thought I've hurt Laura's feelings, etc.
Shoes wearing through. Graffiti.

Lights, fog, cold, river sound, train thunder, dark.
Her warm house opening its doors to me, thank you, thank
    you.

Night movies. Walking in trees, parks, rivers.
Flying above the Fraser to the lunar ghost shed.

Laura & I are going downtown. We are neon
blue. A scream in the ear from a passing car.

We walk, argue, contemplate suicide
a leap into the Fraser / a recurring dream

calm, co-operative
agrees he has an impulse control / anger management problem

Lheidli graves are under us now. Their gravestones are under
    the river
this part of the river is stone dead. Concrete broken on its
    banks.

In singing, I composed a song
dead radio noise in the voice box

they shamed me & showed me the door
& tried to put my head through the window. I did it

that morning at the school
that morning at the school

He was initially quite confrontational and presented with a sense
    of bravado
and a challenging style. He is extremely articulate and seems to
    rely on his verbal skills

to try to get himself out
of difficult situations.

James told me later that he saw the vice-principal's eye, the iris
    had orange
dripping somehow into the blue. I believe him.

It was that cold when there is no snow or wind but hard, inert
    frost
& a layer of ice covers the town. Pavement is slippery.

School lights dim except in narrow halls, where fluorescents
    alternate with black where lights
have failed for some time.

Blaze a spliff, the one I bought that morning
at the school, outside the teachers' lounge during the fire drill.

Did I think I saw
those curtains swish?

Gave him three dollars, to still owe two which I didn't know but
    guessed I would not pay
(swearing up & down I would)

John in the back parking lot of Prince George Senior Secondary School

blue doors opening
in the self

his brown hand with the black coat cuff taking my money,
     handing
me a sad, skinny joint.

In Grade 1 I punched him in the nose. First, he punched me &
     made my nose bleed—can't
remember at all why—so I punched him

made him bleed. Then we put our arms around each other's
     shoulders, smiling
& walked around like that, laughing.

His shiny green jacket with the gold
stripes & now a drop of my blood.

Two dollars in overcast courtyard
students still spilling past.

We never talked until high school. Our fists handed off
the trade, money for dope, & headed back to different alternate
     ed classes.

When they asked, I turned
you in without a blink

try to remember what it was really like to be there
but it disappeared before it even happened the first time (that
     was not the first

glasses off hit in the head by mystery teens
with rock at age seven while playing in field

philosophical observations that appear on a swing set & all the
    friends the pretty girls
the longhairs & their ice cream in the park & their train rides
    in a circle & it's cool

when I was in the ward they wouldn't let me call my Mom. She
    called me, too, but
the nurses wouldn't let her talk to me. Might be upsetting.

Mother reports she has been trying
to get help for John for quite some time.

I became a riff of my own voices in layers like leaves
in spring after the snow is gone

I can see all my different colours, green gold brown
rotting there, becoming something else in time

Simon:	*. . . went out of my way, or done anything whatsoever to prepare for this. I haven't even bothered to like try to recollect the story in my mind ahead of time to see if I'm missing any big chunks.*
John:	*I thought you probably hadn't — I was kinda hoping you wouldn't . . .*
Simon:	*[laughs] So I used to actually, I used to actually tell this to people when they would, y'know, people, when they're sort of trying to create connection and aren't really sure where to go will often ask you to tell a story. I've often told this story when people ask me to tell a story, which I like, because it's not, y'know, it's a very long story, which I think is very awkward to people. And it's also not a particularly — the experience of listening to the story isn't necessarily joyful.*
John:	*No, uh . . .*
Simon:	*[laughs] Right. And, but, it's such a good story, that I have this idea that when I do tell it to people, that by the end they'll be thankful.*
John:	*Mmm. All right . . .*
Simon:	*If, y'know, they're willing to sit and listen to the whole thing.*
John:	*And receive that, yeah . . .*
Simon:	*Um. And I usually told the story with a preface of "this is a story about the worst day ever."*

John: [laughs] Right.

Simon: [laughs] And, uh, let's see . . . so. The story begins when my friend John Stevenson was in twelfth grade, was in his last year of, of high school, of the high school he was going to in Prince George. It was in November. The summer before had been just a lot of partying, and getting back into the routine wasn't going smoothly, and he was . . . He woke up in the morning, and he had to wake up early cause he had to go to get tested. For this, uh, because he had slept with somebody that he wasn't entirely sure about, or, uh, happy about afterwards, and he had this anxiety about, that he might have an STD. So the day began with this, y'know, invasive process of something, y'know, being put up his urinary tract or whatever, in order to test for this thing, that y'know, either way, he was going to have this uncomfortable experience, and y'know, best case scenario was that things didn't get worse . . .

we're smoking & smoking
hash oil on cigarettes

this will be dissolved into the text
a drug & you can see some discolouration

"what can I say, I abused what power was given to me
& it was like a dream & I'm still dreaming"

Because it is a transformation.
She reached into his elastic waist

waking up again together with tar tea in
the bedside cup—cigarette butts in water

"If I could, I'd have a cigarette that would burn forever
I'd smoke instead of breathing"

she says something, but "I can't quite
hear you" speak closer to the telephone

trying to wrap his hands around a prose inseparable
from corrupt Eros smoking on the edge of his bed

when we came
to the group home to get her

gone. We ate acid by the fence.
There is a little picture on it

we leave a message for her with the staff
"the fire truck at midnight"

when it kicks in, the movie frames
snap in the pickets

we return to my house where my mom
has cleaned my room & has questions

"let's talk about it later
bye"

(what brings me back to this
scene over & over?

*Insight into his own behaviour seems lacking, but
interestingly, he takes full responsibility*

to see the fire truck at midnight
in the park, running & howling

with the wild teens smoking & laughing
& she doesn't show

& her Catholic name disappears
into memory's blank stare

group home kids can escape
in a pinch. They all do it.

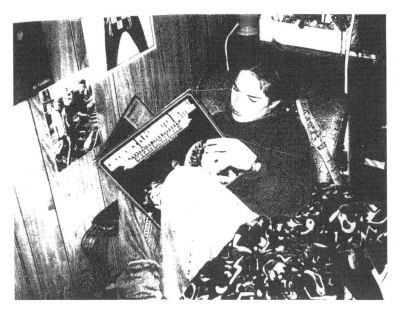

Laura in John's bedroom

saw Laura in the shadow of the Urban
Coffeehouse where speed kids wait

for highs to wear off
so they can go home

the results of the test are never
one hundred per cent. How much

blood can they take? A red
Hawaiian shirt, asleep on the floor

tempted to die of exposure, even
in the summer night

there is no significant medical history
according to his records and his mother's account

and there is no history
of seizure disorder or of significant head injury

dreamed I went to hell &
it was a crowded hospital without windows

I am not a prisoner
(scramble shame memories to make them disappear

I am a patient
(what's the difference

thought flow, form,
and content seem normal.

Path behind Seymour Elementary School

The chain link fence surrounds the grounds of Seymour Elementary school. I don't use the gate; I walk around to the left of the fence where the ground narrows above a short, steep slope darkened by black-green pines. The narrow ground is icy & dirty with pine needles & mud, half frozen, crunching & sinking under my weight. Under my feet. The frozen ground tries to send me down the slope in my grey women's winter coat, it's wool, from Woolworth's. A long coat with a red pine needle or two stuck near the bottom. Near the cold ground. My sneakers try to slip & fail. I pass the chain link to the taller white paint-peeling fences, where I can see snow rotting in yards through the cracks & knots. I hold a cold, sticky tree, then a fence, over difficult places in the path where the ground recedes. I pull myself along, twice put my hand in a thorn bush to move the quickest, most direct way to Prince George Senior Secondary. But this isn't so quick. My last smoke is gone, burned, breathed, I inhaled its medicine. With no more smokes, cold & slipping, thorns in my hands, cold feet in itchy wool socks with holes, & a women's coat, hair in my face dyed black, creeping along the edges of these middle-class fences on the way to class. Thorns in my hands. The wind nipping at me with its nonsense words in the grey morning. Through & along the black pines until I sleep a little, slip a little in the falling path, the narrow sky & quiet houses, highway hissing mechanically somewhere below me.

Every day for years, since I was a little kid even, I get anxious in the morning or in the car or even before I wake up because I have to go to school & I don't want to go. My stomach hurts in the car & I feel like I want to puke. I put metal on the stereo while I get dressed most days. Should stay home & play guitar like I did on correspondence when I was kicked out the last time. I'm only going for a little while today, I don't even know why I'm going. Just put in an appearance today, so glad you could join us Mr. Stevenson. I could just go upstairs & play one of the crummy school guitars in the hall with the other guys. After lunch.

Opens up into the street at last, ice on the ground, in the wind. I move across this ground to the left, toward the flat, brown brick building I can now see far across the empty street, to the blue double doors into the school, past the icy, muddy parking lot with its rust-bucket trucks & cars, gravel, shop-wing noise. No smoking kids now—class must be in. Crunch on the ground with my flat-soled shoes. Opening the heavy doors, the rush of warm air sucked outside where it is airless & bleak. Shoes squeak on smooth floors underneath fluorescent buzz in narrow, windowless white brick halls. Doors pass. Into the school. Brush my hair out of my face. My soft, red face, stinging as it warms. The soft, short black hairs on my face. Dark brown. My glasses are fogged & I can't see except light & I can't see my breath now that I'm inside. Past the cafeteria to the class. Halls mostly empty. A boy approaches. Short hair, glasses, thin blond beard, broad face & smile. He says, "Hey, man. I bet you thought I forgot, but I didn't." & he holds up his cigarette pack, opens it, & he hands me a smoke. "What? Oh, yeah."
I gave him one yesterday. I reach into the pocket of my long grey coat & pull out a piece of purple paper: a flier for a poetry reading. I put it back in my pocket as I pull out my black, empty cigarette pack with the gold foil letters. I take the cigarette from him, saying, "Hey, thanks, bro. I was all out." A Player's Light. "No worries," he tells me, as I put the cigarette in my pack, & he walks off down the hall, leaving me standing there in front of the cafeteria where a small number chats, milling, spraying milk at each other. I put my pack in my pocket, thinking I'll save it, & turn back toward the hall to class. Slightly urgent.

difficult to recover from the things that happen
to us it doesn't happen all at once but

the things that happen to us / the ink on the wall
on the sign & to sit on the swing & imagine

he believes that he is quite capable
of working through his own problems

and that he should be left alone
to do that

my band is warming up
or taking an hour to tune

here is a 60 Hz hum, here is house power
all on its own as garage howl

attack of double kick
with wooden beaters

fuzz grunge cosmic meltdown
& rainbow puke in the dust

whip me up a sludge pancake
for a microdot eye ziggurat

snap out of a gonzo head
space titan your asteroid belt

giving away free backyard undercuts
swinging locks in the breeze with an underduck

amp edging off the chair
what with the magnetism & all

frayed jeans, light them little
strands & burn 'em off

but solid-state is cheap
& reliable

tie-dyed violence
out of the corner of your stare

so fuck off
on freedom's cartoon eagle

baby
mine

until Mom cleans up
after you

During hospitalization
the patient comes across

as an articulate young man
with a facade of bravado

but who in fact suffers
from very poor self-esteem.

Rock out with crushing riffs, basement woes
parlayed into hard metal to scrape away

everything as I knew it would be, only
without any pain, man

"this is rock n' roll,"
says the sister

(we shook the whole house with the drop-tuned double-kicking racket & you could hear us all the way over at the 7-Eleven according to my mom who heard us there on the way back from McDonald's when she stopped with my sister there to get a scratch & win but didn't win but heard us all the way from over there, me screaming away & I had this necklace on with black plastic beads that Brendan said made me look like Richie Blackmore from Deep Purple who I thought had a monobrow & I didn't so I was more handsome I thought but he was from Deep Purple & how badass was that & I had this thin blue shirt from the thrift shop I was wearing & we rocked out so hard & all the girls loved us & I felt insane I couldn't breathe but it was manic glee & when the song was over & everyone was happy I ran upstairs by myself & lay on the floor & closed my eyes & I thought "never forget how this feels" never forget how this feels & I will never forget & then I wondered if it was a good feeling but it didn't matter because I felt the beautiful power rocking in my soul & that any girl would fall in love with me if I looked her in the eyes & especially Laura I thought & I thought my hair was also perfect while dishevelled because only effortless perfection is real & all the rest is just a style but my long curls were my secret weapon but I didn't have to think about it I just went downstairs & Laura & everyone was like "let's get out of here & go get some dope" because the jam was over but the night was just beginning)

Simon: *Um, so, he got to school late. And, um, school at that point was largely consisting of — y'know, the classes he bothered going to, and, um, Alt Ed, which was basically a class where it didn't matter whether you bothered going to it or not. Ah, there wasn't really much in the way of, I mean, Alt Ed, Alternate Education, and yet there really wasn't that much of the education part, it was mostly just alternate. It was a class full of people who, it was more trouble to keep them in class than not, and, so, a class where they didn't have to try as hard. And this wasn't, y'know, by any means because John couldn't have been good at school, or wasn't capable of doing the work, because of, y'know, intellectual reasons, he was one of these people that seem to know that they aren't particularly suited for high school . . . um . . . I don't know if anybody ever really is or has been, but he happened to know he wasn't. So, he wasn't interested in going, et cetera.*

John's band performing at the Legion Hall

Red reflection of my face in black truck stop window
sign light—zombie power to the max

pixilated noise rushing at my eyes over 15th Avenue
& I feel it so tired, so tired of being high

rushing into my open & closed eyes.
Imagine own face again & again, different forms own

forgotten face while stoned. Collapsing lung, can't
think in a crawlspace, smoke, fire

to the dirty mirror: "Oh, *you* again."
Can't sit or stand or be well, oh God.

Knife in the drawer to feel safe again in my hand
checking behind all the doors 3:21 AM.

We did rock yes we did the amps & the drums all around us
& the kids under the stairs were getting fucked & fucked up

wait for her with friends in the sunset
along a fence outside Yew St. group home.

She never shows. We plan to meet
to reel back in a movie

mirrors on mirrors like the three-way folding
mirrors closed around me as a child

in Sears, staring into the innumerable
self-images all angles & planes

into & under clothing racks, a brat
while family searches in rising panic.

Adjustment disorder with disturbance of conduct. Query
underlying dysthymia. Query

underlying major depression
with masked symptomatology.

Voices high
on Connaught Hill

irreversible transition to experience a nightmare
sexualized in hell

grease bomb moon food truck stop
Martian waitress cops drunks. $1.79 food yum!

Took their smoke & ran, went ape, swung arms
when they follow I run farther

graves we are walking on Lheidli graves
& none of it is fun until I forget

DRUG HISTORY:

The patient smokes cigarettes, does not use alcohol, but admits to daily use of cannabis, particularly in the past few months. He does not consider this to be a problem because he thinks he is not smoking enough of it, using only one reefer a day. He has used other drugs experimentally, eg. LSD, but this is not a problem at present.

Village Towers Apartments

Karen sat on the brown dirty plastic chair in the lobby of Village Towers Apartments, asked me, "You really think you're going to kill yourself?" Her brows knitted, her hands working. Folding & unfolding. "Yes. This time I actually think I might do it." A car passed by, headlights glaring off the black of the window glass in which I could see us, Karen & me, in the window's black reflection. Surge of an adrenaline destructive guilty sad feeling in my belly as I thought of Laura upstairs, up the elevator, closed in the dark in the bathroom in Karen's dad's 11th floor apartment. I imagined our friends at the bathroom door, trying to get her to come out by asking her questions she would not answer, promising this or that.

We had all hung out drinking Karen's dad's coffee all day like we had done the day before & so on, all summer. We had a conversation about dreams, goals, plans, the future, work, being grownups, & I had said that I had no future & I planned to die before I turned eighteen. Everyone argued with me, pleaded with me, & I got more determined, more worked up, until I thought I might have to just jump right off the apartment's 11th floor balcony. Laura flipped and threw a chair. She had strictly forbidden me from talking suicide on the grounds that she found it upsetting. She said I was "acting fucking stupid" & she stood up & went & locked herself in the bathroom. So Karen & I were waiting there, sitting on the hard dirty brown plastic chairs in the lobby of the Village Towers Apartments, hearing the laundromat dryers churn on the other side of the wall, waiting for the ambulance I phoned to come & take me to the funny farm.

The ambulance took so long I almost changed my mind. After we arrived at the hospital, I waited in the emergency waiting room, docile. I contemplated asking for a pen & paper so I could write poems, thought better of it. The nurse at the desk eventually called me over. She asked many questions, like, "Have you ever been diagnosed with depression or any other mental illness? Have you ever attempted suicide before? What was the method?" "No, yes, hanging." But I didn't say I tried hanging in a way that would never work. I could always stop myself at the last minute. Only tempt fate a little. I was in a part of the emergency area I hadn't been to before. There was a tall, curving desk with a white top. I looked around sheepishly at the sick, injured, ugly, dangerous crowd in the waiting room, waiting in line behind me, standing in my pale blue spring jacket, ashamed, positive I was suddenly okay. I waited, sure I was feeling altogether ever so much better except for hospital anxiety.

The front desk nurse pointed with her pen, told me to go down the hall & sit in a smaller waiting room all surrounded by beds with hanging curtains around them. There was a pregnant girl already sitting there who had a ponytail. She looked at me blandly with tired eyes. A nurse came to talk to me. She said her name was Carla & she was maybe fifty & thin with curly grey hair. She was not wearing a uniform, but a blue cardigan & pink slacks. She had glasses & she spoke softly but definitely to me. She asked me why I was so upset & if I thought I was going to kill myself & if I wanted to stay there at the hospital & was I depressed & was I taking anything for it & my answers were really weak, I didn't really know any of the answers to her questions except that the stark white building scared me & I really just wanted to go home, but I didn't tell her that, just tried to answer without lying, because I also wanted to answer her questions as best I could. Carla saw that I was not serious about killing myself. I guess I knew, too, but I kept holding out. She asked me, "Have you thought seriously about getting some counselling?" & I said, "Yes," I would do that, I thought; I would talk to my family doctor. "You know," she said, "even if it seems like a waste of time, it's probably not. Your counsellor will really try to help you." "I know," I agreed, "I know, it's just hard because I don't want to talk to some stranger about my problems." Carla understood things. She blinked behind her glasses. She sent me home, making me agree not to hurt myself.

Outside the hospital it was night & there were smokers coughing in the orange light above the dark glass doors. I walked through them & their smoke & down the hill in the direction of home.

Exterior view of the Prince George Regional Hospital
Psychiatric Intensive Care Unit

imagine myself crying wrapped in own arms
under clanging metal hospital bed

unzipping fly
buzz in the room

telephone slowly destroyed by picking
over anxious calls

underground scene pink shirt white
pants white shoes black stripe

seen it myself at a young age
Narcissus trampled under own feet

we don't make love, we rub
our bodies together

I am not an unusually
honest person

young men with tight fists
& shirts in truck

goon eyes look out like "what
the fuck, man?" He says

& for a minute we are just children again, seeing
everything as we knew it would be, quiet, smiling

to ourselves, a source of income
& outgo, an index

with some revealing answers I wish
I could hide from counsellor eyes

could choose anything still while
health lasts (only slight hearing loss

could become well could become
well could become well still could

happens so fast it's gone
once you realize

& I have disappeared too far
flirt with the high ledge, come back

of course I went out there
but I never believed I'd do it

didn't realize how I'd done it already
by going out there

dropped an empty wine bottle
off the 11th floor balcony

didn't break, just bounced
& made a hollow ringing sound

took a long time to fall
to see what could've happened

knowing many lines will be cut
& any one could have told all

in the mirror forgotten stories moon
landscape dream crawlspace secret library

or the grave
for what's unsaid

under daily threat
of getting asses kicked / having to kick someone's

telling glamorous lies
leisurely rewriting them

PERSONAL HISTORY:
*His records show no
significant problems in
early development or with
developmental milestones.
He has been a good student
and is currently in Grade
10, although he is enrolled
in Grade 11 and 12 classes
as well. It seems he has
been placed in an Alternate
Education program not due
to poor performance, but
due to poor attendance. It is
not clear whether his school
performance has deteriorated
this semester, but it is quite
clear that he has had impulse
control problems at school.
There was an incident in
September when, after some
kind of altercation, possibly
with the same vice-principal,
when he threatened to burn
the school down.*

I was walking away quickly
from where the guys were
going to fight the kid with the
stupid fake punk haircut who
was a real asshole because
Mr. Gerhardt had just come
up & he was like, "What's
going on here?" & no one
moved, standing opposite in
groups in the hall & Gerhardt
walked into that space in the
middle & he looked at me like
this was my scene & I just
left, I went out of the doors
& he followed me. & he left
the scene where the fight was
about to begin to follow me
& asked me, "Where are you
going?" As I walked past the
front of the school, away with
my shoulders squared saying,
"Home, man! Leave me alone,
I'm not doing anything!
Look, I walked away, see?" &
he stopped & his eyes cleared,
& he stood straight & he said,
"Oh, so you have nothing to
do with this now, right, are
we clear?" & I kept walking &
I said, "Goodbye."

John's house

Simon: *Um. So, he went to school, and, um, he tried to find*
. . . er, no, he went to, ah . . . the first thing he did
was to go to class. And he went to the Alt Ed class
that he was scheduled for at that time, and . . . he
arrived, and there was a substitute teacher, which,
in Alt Ed, was even more of an excuse not to go,
because there was even less of an incentive. So he
decided to wander the halls to find someone to
smoke a joint with.

PICU
(there was a camera in the bathroom)

attempted:
narrative coherence

other factors contributing to length of patient's stay
overnight observation:

Quiet
Room

self-narrative text
forgetting this or that detail

somebody following you around
with an eraser

crooked lines in the forehead
seep eventually into thoughts

bad haircuts
$10 / head

sing to me now & tuck me in
cold warm feeling in the room

it's difficult to write a line
more like a compound fracture

assembling a box of letters
a box of memories

when contradictions start to speak up, stroke
their hair & coo to their weariness

various words
the Doctor said   gestures

blinking strobes in your eyes
to see if he is seizure-prone

this test is pass
or fail

you'll hear the way they talk, but
you'll never believe it

yes, I did repeat lies
that were used against me

life itself is the prisoner now
& it will make its bloody escape

she came through the door several times
making restrained, murderous gestures

while we laughed crazy
or even harder

& I found out how bad
feeling bad can feel

temper   temper
        tantrum   tantrum

Simon:	*No, that's not right. There was a fire bell that happened first. And he went out to . . . and when he was out, outside . . . the fire bell went out, and so he sort of wandered outside with all the other kids, and while he was outside, he ran into this guy that he knew, and, y'know, asked him if he had a joint. And the guy gave him a joint. And he was going back inside, and he ran into somebody else, the order of events is a little off, and ran into somebody else who, uh, um, he had bummed a cigarette from earlier. From this guy, and, y'know, John got a cigarette out of his pack, and gave it back to this kid. And . . . or maybe it was the other way around, the kid was returning a cigarette to him, whatever, so he pulls out his packet of cigarettes to put the cigarette into, and also pulls out this little purple flier for a show —*
John:	*Poetry reading.*
Simon:	*For a poetry reading. And what you have to know, if you happen to be an American, like many of the recipients of this story have been, is that, uh, Canadian ten-dollar bills are purple. So he put the cigarette into the pack and wandered around for a bit trying to find someone to smoke this joint with. And, uh, lo and behold, the person he happened to find was James, his younger brother, who also happened to be wandering the halls, and James was up for smoking, smoking a joint, so they sort of wandered off together to the, sort of the back forty behind the school. Where there were some trees, still, and, y'know, started to smoke this joint together.*

I came up the stairs & James was at the top, he was just coming down. So I said "James! Wanna go smoke up?" "Oh, hey, John, yeah! Do you have one?" "Yeah. It's a pinner, but it'll take the edge off." "Sweet." & we turned & walked back down the stairs, the little black plastic stair grip pyramids under our feet, the grey concrete walls around us, to the blue double doors of the shop wing & out into the November cold. We went through the parking lot to the thin patch of woods, the "magic forest" as it was known to us. We came to a place where a pine about a foot through had fallen down & was still leaning on its stump. We could see the blue double doors of the shop wing through the frosty pines. I pulled my black cigarette pack out of my pocket & took out the little joint. "Yeah, sure is a pinner," smirked James. "Don't look a gift horse," I told him. "Have you got a lighter?" I asked him. "All I got is matches." So James took out his green bic. Sparked it up & tasted it & passed it to him, not too bad, not much good, didn't get real stoned. Put the little roach in my pack. So we sat there for a minute on the fallen-down pine & looked around. I reached into my pack, pulled out, looked at, held, & lit the smoke I'd been saving. Handed it to James, who took a drag, handed it back. "Thanks, John." I kicked some dirty snow & then I felt this sense, this undeniable feeling. There was somebody watching me with a pair of binoculars & it was somebody pretty bad. I told James, I said, "Whoa, I just got this bad, paranoid feeling. Is there anybody by the doors?" & we looked all around & we couldn't see anyone. But still those binocular eyes hovering in my mind out of sight. "You're just paranoid, man. There's nobody here. Besides, it's too early in the morning to run." I kind of laughed at that. "Yeah . . ." So we stood up, stretched, & started back through the trees over the parking lot & through the blue double doors. The halls were silent. Except for our falling steps. In the main building, a long way down the hall, we could see Mr. Gerhardt & Big Bill coming. They were intent on us. They were staring, pointing, striding toward us. James played it cool. I tried, too, but my heart started racing & racing & I saw the binocular eyes & I started to panic but I kept walking, kept pace with James, until they were right there. & Mr. Gerhardt said, "John, go to the office immediately." I said, "How come?" & he said, "Go. Right now. If I get there & you're not there, big trouble," & he made a tight-mouthed face. Bill, standing there, tense, his huge arms hanging over his barrel sides. James looks at me, panicked, sort of an invisible shoulder shrug. Without another word, I walk down the hall toward the office. I don't look back. "You, come with us," I hear Gerhardt say to James.

Simon:	*He immediately assumed that he'd been caught with his brother smoking pot, and that his anxiety had sort of been fulfilled. Um. So he gets brought to the office and doesn't really think twice or think to ask any questions about why he's being brought there. But then James, um, ends up being taken somewhere else, and John's left waiting there for the principal to show up. Um.*

John finds out later that what had happened to James was that he'd been taken to the boys' bathroom by the principal, and, y'know, the principal turns to him and says, "Who are you?" and James says, "I'm James, I'm James Stevenson, I'm John's brother," and he says, "No, you're not! Who are you?" and he says, "I'm James, I'm James Stevenson, I'm John's brother, I've been going to this school for the last three years," or whatever, and the principal says, "John doesn't have a brother! I've never seen you here before in my life. Get out of this, get out of here, and never come back."

And James took that as an excuse to skip school for the day, and he's like, "Sure, fuck, fine, I'm leaving," and he took off.

James

Simon:	*Meanwhile, John's waiting in the office, waiting in the office . . . bored out of his skull and wishing that at least something would happen, even if it was the principal coming to tell him off for smoking pot at school. And nothing happens and nobody comes so eventually his real Alt Ed teacher happens into the office, and John says, "Hey, I've been waiting here for the principal to show up, and he said he was going to be right back, and it's been like, I don't know, forty-five minutes and I don't know where he is, I think he's doin' somethin' else, and is it, I just want to do my work, is it all right if I just go back to the classroom and do some work?"*
	And she was like, "Yeah, fine, sure." Y'know. "You can do some work. Sounds good."
	So he goes back to the classroom, where the principal promptly finds him, now pissed that he has left the office where he had intentionally left him to stay, drags him back to the principal's office where he proceeds to tell him that he has an eyewitness claiming that he, John, had been selling crack to, or cocaine or something, to one of the other students, of the school . . . crack, cocaine . . .
John:	*Actually, he just said that he thought it was a joint . . .*
Simon:	*A joint, oh, right, selling drugs . . .*
John:	*Yeah, selling drugs . . . it was all the same.*

Simon:	To somebody at the — to somebody else at the school, and John, y'know, he's thinking, *Was it during the fire bell, when somebody else sold me a joint? Like, how could have thought that I was selling* . . . And then, then he said, he says, "I don't know what you're talking about, I don't have anything on me, I don't, you can check my pockets, y'know," but he's like, "No, we distinctly saw it, y'know, you gave somebody — you gave somebody drugs, and then you took a ten-dollar bill from them."

And John proceeds to empty his pockets, upon which they find a box, y'know, a pack of smokes and this purple piece of paper from the poetry reading. Y'know, John says, "This must've been what you saw, the 'ten-dollar bill,' I don't know, and look, it's just an advertisement for a poetry reading, and look, there's nothing in this box of cigarettes."

He opens it, and, y'know, the principal takes it and empties it out, and a tiny, tiny, little pin-sized roach from the joint they had just finished smoking falls out onto the table. And the principal looks at and he says, "Well, y'know, we may not be able to bust you for selling, but these are obviously drugs, and there's a zero tolerance here, so you're definitely suspended, and I'm going to do everything in my power to make sure you're expelled."

I found five owls
in the woods with James

we came upon their clearing
to find them perched

quietly on the sparse trees
snow patchy on the ground

one in the centre had horns
on his head

we eyed one another for a minute
& then, one by one, they flew away

into the trees
into the air

Glasses off, I turned to face the open door & he said, "Hey, John—you ever gone ten rounds with a jalapeño?" & sprayed pepper spray into my eyes. There was a hiss. It went in my eyes & started hurting bad fast. I won't give them the satisfaction of hearing me cry out, I thought. I couldn't open my eyes, I squirmed & fell back & tried to rub my eyes but my hands were cuffed behind my back. I made a little yelp. My eyes were burning & stinging & the hurting was becoming more & more intense until I thought it would not become more intense but I was wrong & I tried to open my eyes but they couldn't & I got so scared & sticky water started to gush & leak out of my eyes all over my face & my hair stuck to it.

Voices on the radio asking unintelligible questions. I writhed in my seat in the back of the car. My forehead felt flat where I had smashed it into the window. There was an ache there. Eyes were burning & itching & I tried to reach up but my hands were cuffed behind my back. I reached to try to rub my eyes, rubbed them with my knees. The two silent men drove me along. I mapped where we were by the turns I felt the car take, I could see the map lines, could not make the map work & could not decide if turns were left & right by the light as it went in & out of my eyelids & the falling back & forth across the seat as the momentum of the car changed & I whined & cried because it stung & I couldn't see & I was afraid because the car kept moving & stopping & no one said anything except the crackling radio. Over. The thrum of the motor.

There came a stop longer than the others. The car was turned off. There were door thumps & the weight in the vehicle changed. I tried to sneak a glance but there was no hope. My door opened & the cold hit me in the face. I was pulled out with my crying, draining eyes sticking the hair to my face & I was pulled along, dragging my feet in the parking lot gravel, dragged & pulled into order by the rough hands of the buzzcut men, the crewcut-headed, silent, angry men. & I was pulled along & pushed into the sweaty warm air that struck me with rancid tepidity, the smell of sick people & medicine. Disembodied voices floated on the air that hurried past my hair in the sticky halls of the bad-smelling place where I was, but could not see. I was turned according to where I was supposed to walk & pushed along. I kept trying to see but it hurt to open my eyes so I would have to stop before I could try again.

Then I was stopped. I came into a room & I could open my eye a small crack. There was off-white that used to be white & an orange chair. Immediately it was blurred away. All of it was blurred because my glasses were off. On my hand I could feel the orange chair that had crisscrossing fabric that was coarse. My hands were in metal links behind my back where they could cause no one any more trouble for now. The door was closed & I heard the men sit down across from me on coarse chairs. The metal frame of the chair was cold & smooth. I felt it through the rip in the knee of my jeans. I was sitting. The pain in my eyes was present but lesser. Outside the door came a muffled sound walking past every so often until I heard a sound that made me laugh inside but only inside the sound of my thoughts. My eyes were beginning to die down unless I tried to open them. The inside of my eyes looked black & red with some other patterns emerging. My eyelids were beginning to become stuck closed together.

"Oh my God, is that an O.D.?" "No, a suicide attempt." "Oh my God." I had to laugh inside at these poor women, these muffled nurses through the glass, to whom I was a shock. But it was not a suicide attempt. They were misguided. They were misguided in the extreme. I didn't do this to myself. I didn't. I put a belt around my neck & I tied the leather belt, the Italian hand-tooled leather belt with its little flowers & painted birds, its tiny menagerie, I started to tie it to the rail of the stairs in the hall by the upstairs gym at the school & I looked stupidly at the concrete wall by myself in a rare moment of peace but then I decided that this was fucking stupid & that I can't let them win & this is nothing to kill myself over because they can't kill me with my own hands. & all the voices & the moments came pouring over me in buckets & my sister was there, blue open eyes, & she was very small & the people I suddenly remembered were smiling at me because they loved me & my Grandmother never stopped believing I was perfect, no matter what I ever did, & she smiled, & the school woman came rushing up to me with her short white hair & her eyes were beady wide & empty & she made her ungainly bound & she screamed at my face "we're only trying to help you!" & I screamed at her & my eyes became hot with anger & probably turned red like cigarette cherries in their black skull hollows & I screamed "get the fuck away from me!" & her face dropped, it changed so fast, & she ran away.

Now it is quiet & I hear the nurse & I open my eyes & it stings bad. I stood up & moved away, I never tried to kill myself. But I stay put while the nurse enters. She says "name?" & I say "John Stevenson" & my voice is a grey, raspy croak & I scare myself. She says "are you carrying any I.D.?" & I say "no" & she says "why not?" & I say "because I'm fifteen" & she says nothing. But I hear the pen scratchy-scratching against the paper that she holds against the clipboard against her breasts. & she asks questions about my mother & my mother's name & about my size & my medical needs & I say "I'd like an eyewash" but none ever comes. The nurse leaves. I can open my eyes a little bit & the pain is less & my face is streaked with large sticky tears & the cop is looking at me like he could just puke & the other one is a wash, he can't see me at all, he is asleep on his feet, & he is blond. & this is what I can see without my glasses. But the dark one says nothing, pointedly. So I ask him, "can I help you?" & he thinks for a long time about my question. He says "can you help me? Can you help me? Do you think this is a fucking fast food restaurant, you're going to get me a fucking cheeseburger? I missed my fucking lunch break because of you, kid. You shut the fuck up." So I shut the fuck up. & I waited in the small, little room across from the two cops. The light one is

Larry & the dark one is Moe—where's Curly? Wait, I must be Curly. My hair is stuck to my face & it is black.

My doctor came in. He said, "Well, you look like you've had a bit of a dust up." He had a Northern Irish accent. I agreed, imagining how I looked. "I hear you've had a suicide attempt. You can sign yourself over to us here, agree to have yourself committed, & you won't have to go downtown with these gentlemen. What do you think?" They took off the cuffs so I could sign. I signed. I kind of laughed & told him, "It's been that kind of day, might as well sign," but he didn't laugh, seemed afraid of the laugh. "Good, well, have a good rest, let me know if there's anything you need." But anything I needed, doctor, you could not provide. I would never ask you. You're a fine doctor. Leave me alone.

A nurse came & led me along the halls to an elevator where I stared straight in front of me. There were fluorescent lights & sick people & friends of sick people & people in green suits & people in orange suits carrying clipboards & paper. All these sights passed by me with a fuzzy halo because my glasses were gone Lord knows where & a disembodied voice naming people's names & telling them where they were needed was appearing & disappearing all around us. I could see everything badly & my eyes felt hot & sticky but my face was dry & tight with dried tears. Behind me were angry cops. They said nothing. When the elevator arrived I got out with the leading nurse & the following cops to a room with a big pale orange door with a narrow reinforced glass window high up on it after a little room where there were four black & white televisions & a silver microphone. The room with the pale orange door was where I was led. She gave me thin green pajamas. I just stood there holding them, not knowing, but then I asked for privacy & the cops grudgingly left the room. I pulled off my torn jeans & my white long johns & my wool socks & my grey wool coat & my black T-shirt which all fell to the floor with a sigh & I put on the cold green pjs & through the open door the dark cop called out "hey, John! Hope you're not trying to hang yourself with your underwear. Hahahahaha!" But he knew I wasn't.

They said their goodbyes & there was a long pause while I considered my surroundings. The fluorescent lights buzzed overhead & made a white pallor. There was smooth pale blue sparkly concrete for walls except for a broad stripe of smooth deep red sparkly concrete. There was a slab that was part of the wall & the floor that raised up like a bed & it had a side corner slab like a bedside table. There was a black box with a video camera eye in the top left corner & on the right was a pale orange door with a small narrow window onto the back hall high up on it. In the ceiling was a metal grill & a fan was blowing evenly behind it. & the lights. I sat down. The cold of the stone cut through the rear of the thin green pajamas. Everyone was gone for now. No glasses or watch.

I imagined the rows of people in the halls who were watching me when the cops carried me out of school & I couldn't see them without my glasses but I could see they were staring & they were silent & there was only the sounds of the radios on the cops belts & the shoes squeaking against the polished school floor & the handcuffs that cut my wrists behind my back & every door we came up to I smashed my face on it & I smashed it again until we came to the front & I decided not to & I told the cop, I said "I'm calm now" & he said "shut the fuck up!" & we went out into the snow & the cold & they pushed me against the police car & they emptied my pockets into the snow & my glasses were gone, back in the hall where they knocked me on my face in the hall where the principals curdled around trying to contain the damage & the cops felt my body all over & they grabbed & squeezed my testicles very hard through my pants & made tears in my eyes & I waited & they pushed me into the car & pepper sprayed me in the eyes & I realized that since that was only lunch, it couldn't be later than 2 PM. I sighed & leaned back against the wall.

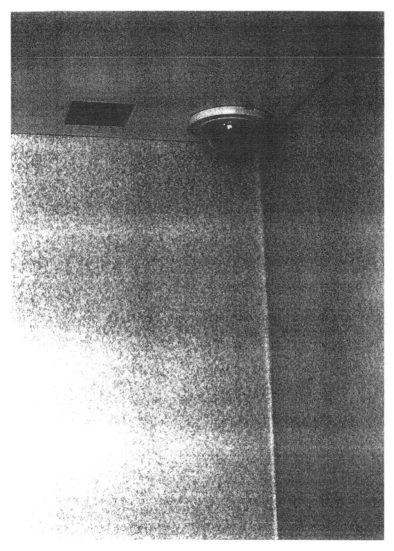

Psychiatric Intensive Care Unit camera

This fifteen-year-old single Caucasian male was brought to the Emergency Room by the RCMP. They had been summoned to the school, where the patient was involved in a disturbance. During the disturbance, the patient tried to hang himself with a belt in the drama class and then resisted arrest, trying to bang his head through the glass windows, and had to be sprayed with mace before being handcuffed and brought to hospital.

He was committed under the Mental Health Act by Doctors Bergman and Murphy, because the patient still seemed angry and reported that he was unable to contract against harming himself.

PRESENTING PROBLEM:

When I saw the patient later that day, he appeared far more subdued than earlier in the day, according to the reports the officers and school staff. The patient told me that the precipitant to his suicide gesture was a false accusation of selling drugs on school property. He was quite angry that the vice-principal believed the report of a handyman who said he saw John passing drugs to another boy in exchange for money. John completely denies dealing with drugs.

There may have been other stressors. Specifically, earlier in the day, the patient had undergone testing at the Public Health Clinic for chlamydia and gonorrhea, due to recent burning during micturition. He is apprehensively awaiting those test results.

Furthermore, the day before, he was threatened by an eighteen-year-old fellow pupil who accused John of hanging around with that fellow's girlfriend.

John feels that, in retrospect, he can understand why the handyman may have thought John was passing drugs. He does remember exchanging a cigarette for a crumpled piece of paper, certainly not money, with another student near the toilets of the school.

As regards suicidal ideation, John informs me that the suicide gesture was an impulsive act, and that he saw no other options. He does appear to appreciate that he overreacted to the circumstances. He admits to similar episodes of overreaction in the recent past, as will be noted below.

About that he was silent.

Simon:	*At one point, bored out of his mind, he decides to start doing push-ups to start working off some of this, like, pent-up, some of this anger, some of this energy, some of this helplessness, feeling like at least he could work some of the energy out. Immediately this voice comes on over the intercom and says, "Stop doing that."*
	So he stops, and he says, "Stop doing what? Push-ups?"
	"Yes."
	"I can't do push-ups?"
	"No."
	"Can I sing?"
	". . . Yes."
	So he sings. And he actually, in singing, starts to compose what ends up being one of my personal favourite John Stevenson songs, which is on his first album, Erasedland Blues . . . *was it* "Solitude?"
John:	"Seclusion."
Simon:	*"Seclusion," right. Oh, that's a brilliant song.*
John:	*Thanks.*
Simon:	*In fact, I think you originally told me this story because I asked you about that song.*

John: *[laughs] Oh, that's great.*

Simon: *But, um . . . So, he just sort of sung the rest of the day away, and spent a lot of time lying on the bench, kinda looking up at the ceiling, walking around, and looking at the walls, and thinking to himself.*

it had a broken string, but next morning
they let me play it here alone (under careful supervision)

& I played the song I'd been writing
under the white lights

and in my opinion the person
is a mentally disordered person.

Later, on a midnight street, stoned with jean-jacketed friends,
    suddenly seeing in the sounds
a premonition voiced by singing chords

& they smiled in the lamp glow of my vision & they walked
with hands in pockets, eyes to street signs

nearer alongside me
hearing the words & music

these may be symptomatic
of depression, i.e. masked depression.

"Seclusion"
by John Stevenson:

(recording cuts
out)

It is also my opinion that   *JOHN STEVENSON*   *requires*
    medical treatment
in a facility, and care, supervision, and control in a facility

for the person's own protection
or for the protection of others (Mental Health Act).

View from the window in the back hall of the
Psychiatric Intensive Care Unit at Prince George Regional Hospital

In the night, Carla came to see me. At first I didn't know where I recognized her from, but then I realized it was from the last time when I was in Emergency, when I came from Karen's place in the ambulance. She said, "I heard you were here, & I came to see how you were doing." "Oh, man," I said, "what a day. I can't wait to go home. The other nurses said I'd be here a long time." She said, "Well, sometimes it can be good to take a break." "I don't want to take a break. I want to go home. What if I miss Christmas in here?" "I brought you something," she said, reaching into her pocket to pull out a Ziploc bag containing my glasses. She handed it to me. I took my glasses out of the bag & examined them. The lenses were intact, but the arms & nose pieces were bent almost flat. I started to fix the frames, careful not to pop a lens out. I said, "Wow! Thanks, Carla, how'd you get them to give them back?" "You have to tell me you won't try to harm yourself, & then you can keep them. I told the nurses I was familiar with you, & that I thought you would agree to my terms." "Okay, yes, sure, I won't hurt myself." "Promise?" "Yeah." I sat on the concrete slab bed in my thin green pjs, looking up at her, looked down to unfold my glasses, & put them on my face, adjusting as I went. Still a bit off, but the lights, the room, sparkles in the concrete, Carla's steady eyes behind her glasses, the curls of her perm all in focus now.

"Do you want to go for a walk?" She asked. I said, "Oh, really? Yeah, could you help me get a smoke?" She left the room, left the door open, & I could see the bathroom through the hall with its warped, dark metal mirror. Can't break it. She talked to the nurse through the open station door where the little TVs were watching. I saw myself see myself in the dark TVs. Carla came back, saying, "C'mon. Let's go downstairs."

In the hall, I could see it was dark outside. She led me through the nurses' station, past the front desk in the third-floor lobby, to the elevator, & we went to the first floor to the smoking room, near the chapel. Bristly-faced men & pasty women & sagging cheeks cough in the miasma of the hospital smoking room. Carla asks, "Do you want me to ask someone for a cigarette for you?" I nod meekly. A large man with a red & white baseball cap gives Carla a smoke, & she asks me "would you like to go outside? It's a bit cold." "Yes, yes, I would, thanks," & we walk down the hall toward the main doors where the orange lights were. More coughing people in the doorway here, parking lot, ambulance area. I bummed a light from a young woman in a nurse's uniform. "I guess I'm probably kicked out of school, huh. Didn't my mom phone? Does she even know where I am? Can I use the phone?" Carla said, "Yes, she did phone, but you can't take calls or have any outside contact, no visitors, not for awhile." "Oh God, oh God . . ." "It'll be okay, it's not forever, it's only to give you time to adjust." "I want to go home." "John, they can't let you go home yet. We think you might be a threat to yourself." "I'm not. I'm not." "It's okay." I breath deep, sigh it out, smoke, watching the smoke leave my mouth, waft away over the parking lot. It was cold enough to see my breath, anyway. I finished & stubbed out my smoke against the wall. "Are you ready to head back?" Carla asked. I looked around at the quiet, smoking people in the orange light. A car passed on 15th Avenue. "Yeah."

"What did Dr. Jalil say to you?" Carla asked. I said, "I don't know . . . he didn't make much sense . . . asked me if I 'read into things.'" Carla nodded. "How's the food?" "Stinks!" & we laughed, headed back up to the seclusion room. "If you need anything," she said, "you can ask for me, & if I'm here, I'll try to help you." "Thanks, Carla."

I sat on the edge of the bed, leaning with my arms crossed, elbows in my hands resting on my knees, nicotine cravings at bay for a while, leaned my head into my arms & started to cry. I cried the long, choking cries with a little sob. My nose was running, & I wiped it on my pajama sleeve. I cried the tired tears of a child whose fight has run out. I saw the faces of the people I'd seen that day. I imagined my mom's anxious eyes, how she'd sleep. They wouldn't even let me call her. &

she was always worried about me—all the stupid things I did. Everything she did was to take care of me and James, but no one was taking care of her. I wondered what happened to James, where he was. He was probably at home, sleeping in his own bed. Thought of all the songs I'd write, where I'd go—Fort George Park, Karen's apartment—the stories I would tell when I got out. Wondered what happened to my clothes, if I'd ever get back into high school. Thought about my band, stupid band, loved the band. Wished sorely that I had a book to read.

I finished crying & dried my face on my shirt, found stray tears in my hair. I lay down on the hard, cold slab, fluorescent lights in my eyes, through my red eyelids, & listened to the fans. They whirred & rattled a little. I thought of my little sister, blue open eyes, started to cry a bit again & then stopped when a nurse came in. She had a blanket & a pillow folded in her arms. "I brought you these, but you can only have them if you promise not to use them to hurt yourself." "Okay, sure, thanks," I said. "Do you want something to help you sleep?" "Like a sleeping pill?" "It's a muscle relaxant." "Sure." She turned around, came back with a paper cup of water & a small plastic cup with a tiny, flat, white pill in it. I took them from her, swallowed them. "That should help you rest," she said. "Thanks," I said, & she left the room. I lay down, pulled the pillow up & put it under my head, grabbed the blanket & pulled it over myself & closed my eyes. Couldn't tell that the pill did anything. Thought for a long time.

Simon:	So John sort of sits back, waits for sleep to take hold, and he lies there, lies there, and eventually he looks up at the window and asks, "When do they turn off the lights around here?"
	There's a moment's silence. "Oh, we don't turn off the lights, we have to keep you under constant surveillance." [laughs]
	"Oh," he says.
	So, after many more hours, he finally ends up falling asleep sometime.

& everywhere all the time the sense
my dreams are continuous with my
    waking

that the stars are a text, the waves
in the carpet, stared into

black cloud at edge of hands
where light falls off, ceases

to reflect, turns inward, inward
on inward on inward to a black

hole, a door under the stairs
unsayable at last, incommensurable

NATURE OF ILLNESS OR INJURY
Attempted

terrible fast clouds
the sky is never

empty, it is always
full of sky

he was able to give
a fair account of himself

emptied boxes to find no scrap
referring to the incident

nothing much at the police
station, hospital, school

back hall minutes
locked doors barred windows
    parking lot

I can sit in this plastic chair
as a reward / planning my escape as
    always

in the distance between what is said
    & meant
empty codes of silence

there is a camera here but
I think I found a blind spot

it's me
        (oh, it's going to snow again

Sitting in ER handcuffed.

Brought in by 2 RCMP

officers. Eyes sore from

Mace spray. Hx of trying

to hang self in drama

room @ school. When

brought out by RCMP

tried to bang head thru

glass windows

Simon:	He wakes up in the morning to the doctor coming in and telling him that basically, in effect, they're not going to keep him in the ward. That despite his actions, and his temper, and his, sort of, characteristics to the contrary, he's not crazy, he's just a jerk . . . more or less. And, tells him to, gives him back his clothes, which are still covered in blood, and his belongings, and he's sent out into the waiting room, where he has to wait for them to un-book him from the psych ward, he's not allowed to go home quite yet, he still has to sit around waiting for the paperwork to end. Which it turns out isn't actually that bad. He gets to meet some of the other people that are also in the ward, he meets a man who is playing, confidently and proudly and joyfully on the piano, full of spirit, and, uh, absolutely no trace of skill whatsoever, but with nothing but, y'know, passion and joy, this sort of tall, Native guy?
John:	Yeah, yeah, a big tall Native guy, like 6'7", big athletic-looking guy, probably about thirty.
Simon:	Right. And then, and he also meets an older woman, who seems to be very pleasant, who tells him that just good things are coming in his life . . .
John:	Oh, yeah, she said that, since I looked older, I would always look the same age.
Simon:	Yeah, that you would always look the same age, and that she wasn't actually in the psych ward, she was waiting for her husband to finish with his kidney dialysis.

John:	*Yeah, which I really . . .*
Simon:	*[laughs] Doubt.*
John:	*[laughs] Which I doubt very much.*
Simon:	*But, y'know, it's as good a story as any, I reckon . . .*
John:	*Yeah.*
Simon:	*So then he goes, and gets his glasses back, and he gets, uh, a cigarette, a box of cigarettes back, which he doesn't remember having, and opens them, and finds that there are a whole multitude of varieties of cigarettes all stuffed into one package, and a note from his friends, who had all donated a couple of cigarettes each to fill this pack, and a card . . . um, two, one? Two cards . . . no, one card, but it was from his friend . . .*
John:	*Liam.*
Simon:	*Liam, who had made this card, it was a cartoon of —*
John:	*Oh, no, that was Karen.*
Simon:	*Oh, Karen made a card, with all his friends on it, and little voice bubbles, and they'd all had gotten to fill in what they wanted to say to him.*

Liam at school

John seems to be an outgoing fellow with a large circle of friends, and seems to enjoy being the centre of attraction. He goes to fairly extreme lengths to maintain his social position, for example getting into more trouble than any of his buddies do, and opposing authority figures more than the others.

"These things came for you in the night, but
we couldn't give them to you until you were released"

a card, a letter, a drawing, a pack of smokes
thank you so much (if only I'd had these last night

it's a cartoon—Karen drew
little pictures of all our friends

*Hi John! This is a quick note, because they probably won't let you
have a long one!*
*Hold in there man, we all love you! We'll get you a smoke
somehow!!*

they all have speech bubbles, & they each
wrote me a message

this fuckin sucks man
Im gonna kick someones ass

the card is from the Art 12 class.
It's an abstract watercolour with grey, white, black, & red

John—take care of your ♥, health +
psyche.

Have a good rest.
Mrs. Feather

inside is a letter, green-grey wash
with black felt pen print. It's from Liam.

*First off I say HELLO! Pricks because the first to read this will be
the 'nurses.' & I think*

your pseudo profession is a scam. Remember Hamlet, Einstein,
*   Galileo, Copernicus?*

[. . .] & never think that I, your friend, agree or believe you
*   should be in there.*
I know you—you know me, they've exercised false judgment

don't let them get to you, we'll all be expectant
of your 'release' from your undeserved confinement.

P.S. my new painting is symbolic of your situation. It is you, I
*   didn't realize it at first*
because nothing had happened yet.

I fold the letter back up & put it in the envelope.
I put the envelope in my long, grey wool coat pocket.

This pack is nearly full. There are maybe two or three each of six
kinds of smokes here. All my friends' brands.

Simon:	*So, with these mementos of his twenty-four hour excursion, he left the psych ward and started walking home. And it was on that walk home that he realized that, uh, that no form of coercive authority would ever be tolerable to him under any circumstance, and that he must do whatever it is that he was meant to do in order to release the . . . uh, release or take . . . power back from those who wish to use authority to do people harm. And that's about all I can remember.*	Walking down the hill, a cigarette in my hand, a breath from my lips I blow out. The cars rush past & dry snow blows around in the cold over the 15th Avenue overpass over Winnipeg Street as I breathe deep the smoke of a John Player's cigarette over the city & away into the day, the same hard white overcast as yesterday, but now I am the freest I've ever felt—guess I don't have to go to school tomorrow either—the freest I've ever been, here walking home in the white cold & the noise I am walking home & I will call my friends & see how they are & did they miss me while I was in the funny farm? &
John:	*Thanks very much, Simon.*	
Simon:	*You're welcome. [tape clicks]*	<u>*DISCHARGE STATUS*</u>: *Alive.*

15th Avenue

<u>CLINICAL IMPRESSION</u>:

The patient does not appear to be a high suicide risk, and he does not appear to be a danger to others. However, one cannot doubt that he has severe impulse control and anger problems which seem to manifest after periods of quiescence of months at a time. It is not clear why this should be so. One possible explanation is that there is an underlying affective disorder, and that he tends to bottle things up for months and then flares up from time to time, after which he is fine again. He may indeed experience similar episodes in the future—or the results of this episode may be enough to cause him to seek further treatment.

I also do not have a clear explanation for why he resents authority figures so much.

silence of an overturned
car

breathe me out
light blue tobacco fumes

"you've got to confront someone about all this"
"we've got a staff sergeant to deal with people like you"

pay phone calls to tell you
I'm free to say

let them do that to me
never again (how to stop them

unfolding letters
smoking to yourself

he backed into that fire hydrant
seven times before he got straightened out

recall the hot night
with Laura in rain

& here a home to go home to
(leave the porchlight on, Mom

how many times to be hit in the face
before I learn to duck?

From Prince George, the last passenger awake
on the night bus to Burns Lake

I want to live
I want to live

James & I both kicked
out of school at the same time

green pajamas go on
uniform days

there used to be a hot tub
in here, that's how come the fan

had a tent set up in his room
for a hotbox chamber

Nintendo addict lies
on couch, controller in hand

or tune up, look west
try to sing something

yes, I (want to) live
& do & on

"I'll come home now
thanks for not hanging up"

sun rises & falls & clouds fly
overhead while I remain

& who will find my remains
& sing them to sleep

& who will sing my sleep
home to unmusical dreams

a star curtain falls
come in come in

Acknowledgements

Of the many friends, family members, mentors, and others to whom I am grateful for everything they gave to me and to this book, my first thanks must go to Rob Budde. I also thank the rest of my MA committee members and teachers: Maryna Romanets, Kristen Guest, Si Transken, Dawne McCance, and Lisa Dickson. I'd like to thank the folks who allowed me to use their photographs or likenesses in this book, including Kathleen De Vere, Lorinda Jackson, Jason Neault, Brandon Moen, Tyler Newton, and Lee Glasgow. Thanks to Naomi K. Lewis, and to everyone at the University of Calgary Press. Thanks to Leona, Jon, and Ashleigh Stewart; and, most of all, thanks to Erin, Ephraim, and Cesárea for all the love and support.

Photo by Lisa Loewen

JEREMY STEWART is a SSHRC Doctoral Fellow in the English Literature department at Lancaster University, UK. His dissertation-in-progress is on Jacques Derrida's "Envois," the Book of Daniel, and dream interpretation. He makes his home in Vancouver, British Columbia with his partner and their children. Read more about his music and writing at jeremystewart.ca.

BRAVE & BRILLIANT SERIES

SERIES EDITOR:
Aritha van Herk, Professor, English, University of Calgary
ISSN 2371-7238 (PRINT) ISSN 2371-7246 (ONLINE)

Brave & Brilliant encompasses fiction, poetry, and everything in between and beyond. Bold and lively, each with its own strong and unique voice, Brave & Brilliant books entertain and engage readers with fresh and energetic approaches to storytelling and verse.